Run-down Racecar

By Sheila Sweeny Higginson
Based on an episode by Kent Redeker
Based on the series created by Chris Nee
Illustrated by Character Building Studio and the Disney Storybook Artists

PaRragon

Bath · New York · Cologne · Melbourne · Delhi
Hong Kong · Shenzhen · Singapore

Doc and Donny are getting ready to race.
Donny puts Ricardo Racecar at the starting line, then Doc picks up a yellow racecar and puts it next to Ricardo.

"After Ricardo beats your car, he's going to be ready for
the Championship-Best-Racecar-Ever race!" Donny says.

"Let's get this race going," Doc says to her brother with a smile. The racers start their engines. And they're off!

Ricardo takes the lead. Donny and Doc watch as the cars zoom round the track.

Donny cheers. "Only one more lap to go before Ricardo wins the race!"

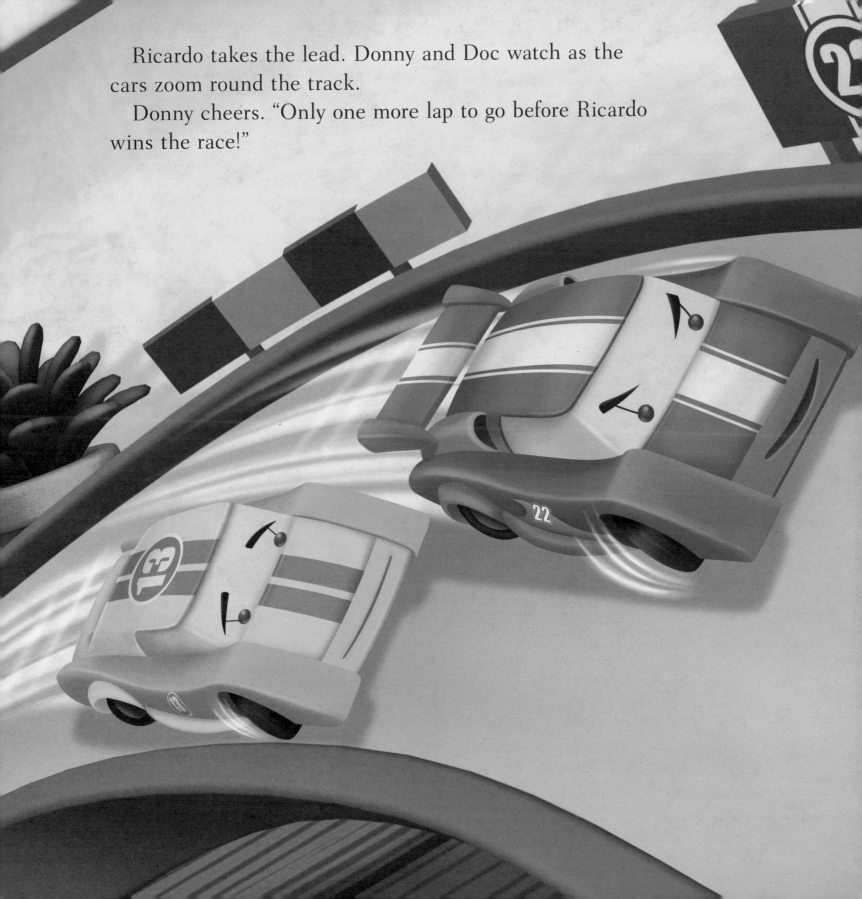

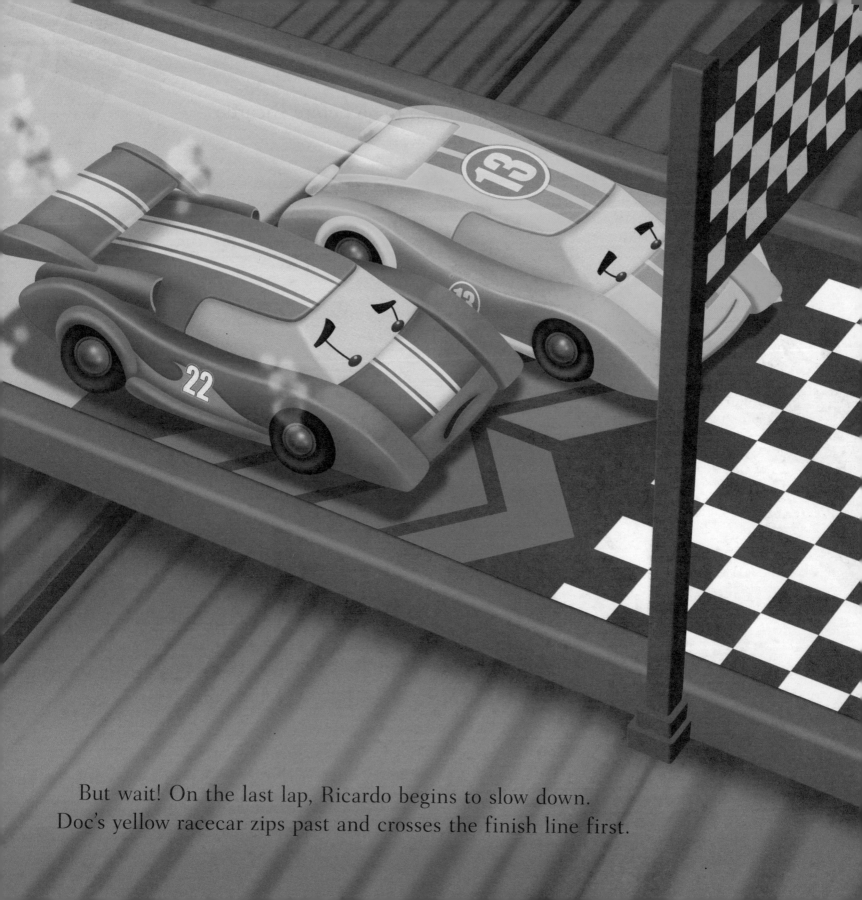

But wait! On the last lap, Ricardo begins to slow down.
Doc's yellow racecar zips past and crosses the finish line first.

"You won!" Donny yells. "That's not possible!"
Donny's eyes fill with tears. He throws the remote control to the floor.
"I'm sorry, Donny," says Doc.

Dad comes in to see what's wrong.
"Donny, I think you need a nap," Dad says.
"But I'm not tired," Donny says. Then he yawns.

"Why don't I see if I can fix Ricardo?" Doc says.
"Good idea, Doc," says Dad.

Dad steers Donny to his bedroom. "If you get some sleep now, it will recharge your batteries," Dad says.

"I'll fix Ricardo before Luca gets here for the big race," Doc adds.

Doc carries Ricardo to her clinic while Donny naps.
Her stethoscope begins to glow. Then magically all the
toys come to life.

Stuffy sees what Doc has in her hand.
"Ricardo Racecar?" says Stuffy. "I'm his number-one fan!"

Ricardo wonders why he is being carried.
He's the greatest racecar there is. Surely he can
race his way across a garden!

"You haven't been going as fast as usual," Doc explains,
"so I'm worried something might be wrong with you."

Ricardo doesn't know what Doc is talking about. He is faster than any racecar around! But when Doc puts him on the ground he sputters and stops.

"But I have a big race today," Ricardo moans.
"Donny is counting on me!"

It's time for Doc to give Ricardo a check-up.
She lifts his bonnet and looks at his engine.
Everything seems okay in there.

"Can you give me a big vroom vroom?" Doc asks.

Ricardo tries, but his vroom doesn't have a lot of power behind it.

Hallie thinks Ricardo looks worn out.

"You raced a bajillion times last night, right?" Doc asks.

"Yes, this is true," says Ricardo. "A bajillion times exactly."

Doc knows what is wrong.

"My diagnosis is No-Vroom-Vroom-atosis!" she tells Ricardo.

Ricardo needs to recharge his battery!

Doc asks Dad to plug Ricardo into the charger.
Before long, Ricardo's battery light turns green. By the
time Donny's nap is over, Ricardo will be all revved up.

Later, Donny's friend Luca comes over to play.
Donny puts Ricardo Racecar at the starting line,
then Luca picks up his car and puts it next to Ricardo.
The racers start their engines. And they're off!

On the last lap Ricardo begins to speed up.
"Go, Ricardo! Go!" Doc cheers.
He zips past Luca's car and crosses the finish line. Ricardo wins!
"Thanks, Doc!" says Donny. "You're the best big sister in the whole wide world!"